Where I live

Where I Live

by Eileen Spinelli

* * *

illustrated by Matt Phelan

Dial Books for Young Readers

DIAL BOOKS FOR YOUNG READERS

A division of Penguin Young Readers Group

Published by The Penguin Group

Penguin Group (USA) Inc., 375 Hudson Street, New York, NY 10014, U.S.A.

Penguin Group (Canada), 90 Eglinton Avenue East, Suite 700, Toronto, Ontario, Canada M4P 2Y3

(a division of Pearson Penguin Canada Inc.)

Penguin Books Ltd, 80 Strand, London WC2R 0RL, England

Penguin Ireland, 25 St. Stephen's Green, Dublin 2, Ireland (a division of Penguin Books Ltd)

Penguin Group (Australia), 250 Camberwell Road, Camberwell, Victoria 3124, Australia (a division of

Pearson Australia Group Pty Ltd)

Penguin Books India Pvt Ltd, 11 Community Centre, Panchsheel Park, New Delhi - 110 017, India

Penguin Group (NZ), Cnr Airborne and Rosedale Roads, Albany, Auckland 1310, New Zealand

(a division of Pearson New Zealand Ltd)

Penguin Books (South Africa) (Pty) Ltd, 24 Sturdee Avenue, Rosebank, Johannesburg 2196, South Africa

Penguin Books Ltd, Registered Offices: 80 Strand, London WC2R 0RL, England

Designed by Lily Malcom

Text set in Garamond 3

Manufactured in China

10 9 8 7 6 5

Library of Congress Cataloging-in-Publication Data

Spinelli, Eileen.

Where I live / Eileen Spinelli ; illustrated by Matt Phelan.

p. cm.

Summary: In a series of poems, Diana writes about her life, both

before and after her father loses his job and she and her family

move far away to live with Grandpa Joe.

ISBN-13: 978-0-8037-3122-6

[1. Moving, Household—Fiction. 2. Family life—Fiction.

3. Astronomy—Fiction. 4. Novels in verse.]   I. Phelan, Matt, ill.

II. Title.

PZ7.5.S68Wh 2007

[Fic]—dc22

2006030971

Where I live

This Is Where I Live

This is where I live—
in the yellow house
with the white shutters.
I'm the one who helped plant
the maple tree in the front yard,
the one who waters
the daffodils in the spring,
who rakes the leaves in autumn.
My room is on the second floor.
See my window?
This morning I looked out
and saw my best friend, Rose,
waving to me.
"Wanna ride bikes?" she called.
The sun was shining,
the sky was so blue,
I thought I could swim in it.
My heart was happy.
It's a good day when
the sky is blue
and the sun is bright
and Rose and I have plans.

New Resident

A wren has made
her nest
in the willow wreath
on our front door.

Now the yellow house
is her home
too.

Note to My Grandpa

Dear Grandpa Joe,

Thank you for
the money you sent.
I am going to buy
paint.
Rose will help me
paint my room.
I'm thinking
midnight blue—
that will go best
with my astronomy charts.
I will send you
a picture of my room
when we finish.

Love,
Diana

Where Grandpa Joe Lives

Grandpa Joe lives far away,
near Pittsburgh.
A six-hour drive.
We don't go very often.
My little sister, Twink,
gets itchy in the car.
Every mile she says:
"I'm hungry!"
"I'm bored!"
"I need to go to the bathroom!"
"Are we there yet?"
I get itchy
just listening to her.
Mostly
Grandpa Joe comes to us.
He's lucky:
no itchy Twink
whining
all the way
from Pittsburgh.

Naming Twink

I gave Twink her name.
It used to be Lucy.
But when she was an infant
I sang to her:
"Twinkle, twinkle little star . . ."
Over and over.
I wanted to teach her
to love the night sky
as much as I did.
When baby Lucy
finally spoke,
her first word
was not
"Ma-ma" or
"Da-da" or even
"No!"
Baby Lucy's
first word was
"Twink."

"I named you."
I remind her
often.
She hates when
I do that.
She folds her arms
across her chest
and pouts and says,
"I named myself!"

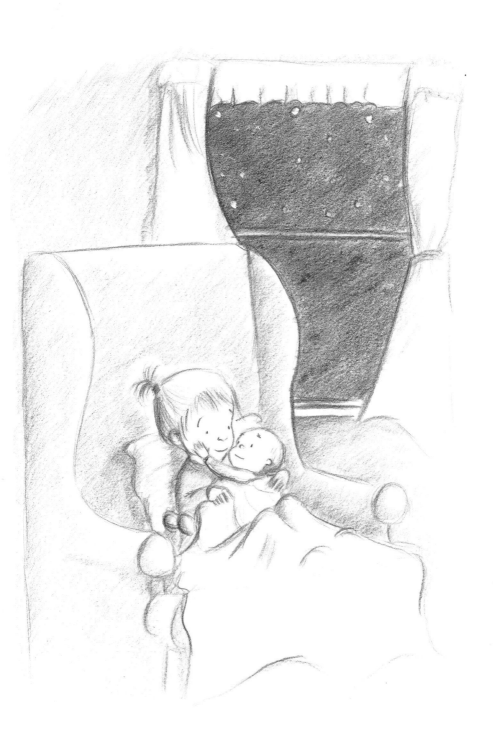

My Six Favorite Star Facts

1. The sun is a star. (In summer I get a starburn.)

2. Real stars do not have five points. Real stars are shaped like balls.

3. There are about 100 sextillion stars in the known universe. (100,000,000,000,000,000,000,000)

4. Every day about 100 tons of stardust land on the earth.

5. The atoms that make up my body were once part of stars. (I'm a star!)

6. Stars shine steadily. They don't twinkle. (Don't tell Twink.)

Dad's Latest

Dad collects jokes
like some people
collect stamps.
Here's his latest:
"What kind of dog
loves to take a bath?"
Twink guesses
"A dirty dog?"
Mom grins.
I shake my head.
"No, Twink," says Dad.
"A shampoodle!"

Back Door

Twink
stands guard
at the front door.
I helped her make a sign.
It says:
BIRD NESTING—
BACK DOOR PLEASE!
She waves it at
the plumber
who comes to fix
the kitchen sink.
She waves it at
the lady
who delivers packages
in a brown truck.
She waves it at Rose.
She waves it at me.
BACK DOOR PLEASE!

One Saturday

Mom takes Rose
and me
to the hardware store
to spend Grandpa Joe's money.
We buy paint—
midnight blue—
and brushes
and a drop cloth.
We stop for donuts.
They'll give us energy
to work (ha ha).
Back home Mom hands Rose and me
a couple of Dad's
old shirts to wear.
Let the painting begin!

Blue

When Rose and I
take a break
from painting,
Twink
sneaks into
my room.
Slappity-slappity
paint on the wall.
Slappity-slippity
paint on the floor.
Slappity-sloppity
paint on Twink.

"Oh no!" I shriek
when I see her.
Rose giggles:
"It's a walking,
talking
blueberry!"

"Water-based paint,
I hope," says Dad.

Mom marches Twink
down the hall.
"Into the bathtub,
young lady."

Twink's tub water
turns blue . . .
dark . . .
dreamy . . .
like a lake
after midnight.

Twink is always
making stuff like this
happen.
Accidentally.

Winner

I can hardly believe it—
I won!
I wrote a poem
for a school contest
about the sun
and
I won!
I won!
I twirl Twink around.
I sing: "I won! I won!"
I can't wait to tell
my parents I won.
They're home!
They get out of the car,
they're coming up the walk.
I grin,
I open my mouth—
Twink runs past me,
shouting, "Diana won!"

This Is My Sun Poem

Sun,
you are like
yellow silk
cut in a circle
stitched against
the sky.
One thread dangles
in the breeze,
says, "Come
climb up into
my golden light.
Be happy."

Twink Responds to My Sun Poem

"It
 doesn't
 rhyme."

My Reply to Twink

"A poem
  doesn't
  have to rhyme."
(Every
  time.)

The Rice Krispies Family

The wren's eggs
have hatched.
There are three
little birds.
Twink has named them:
Snap,
Crackle,
Pop.
After her favorite
cereal.

Proud

My teacher, Mrs. Clifford,
made a poster
of my sun poem.
She hung it
in the hall.
I pass it
every day
on my way to
the cafeteria.
And I try hard not to
beam.

Sleepover

1.

Rose and I play Scrabble.
She wears her purple floppy hat.
The one I call "purpy flopple."
The one I wish was mine.
The one she promises to leave me
in her will.
"It will be all hole-y and moth-eaten by then," I say.
"So." Rose shrugs. "Use it to strain spaghetti."

2.

Rose rolls her eyes.

"*Nebula* is not a word."

"Yes it is," I say, counting up my score.

"What's it mean?"

"It means a kind of cloud in the night sky."

Rose snips: "Use it in a sentence."

"Okay. If my friend Rose looked up at the sky
more often,

she would know a nebula when she saw one."

Rose throws her pillow at me.

"You and your sky!"

3.

We finish the Scrabble game.
I win.
Like always.
(Well—like almost always.)
Rose says: "Let's read each other's diaries."
We do this from time to time.
She gets hers from a box under her bed.
I get mine from my backpack.
"You first," says Rose, flipping her diary
across the bed.

4.

I begin to read:
"Yesterday Billy Borden kissed me
behind the magazine rack in the school library."
My eyes boggle. "He did?"
"No, silly," says Rose. "It's just
more exciting than what really happened."
I ask her: "What really happened?"
"What really happened," sighs Rose, "is that
Billy Borden stomped on my foot
and my big toe still hurts."

5.

"Your turn," I say.

Rose opens my diary.

"Today I saw a cloud that looked
just like a white flower."

Rose yawns.

Closes her eyes.

Soon she's snoring. Zzzzzzzzzzz.

My diary slides out of her hand
to the floor.

"Stop joking around," I say.

"It's not that boring."

But Rose isn't joking.

She really has
fallen asleep.

Something Is Wrong

Dad hasn't told a joke
in three days.
When Mom asked
if he wanted a second helping
of lemon pie
(his favorite food
in the entire universe
including nebulas),
he said, "No thanks, honey."

Mom isn't laughing
like she usually does
(only once, really—
when Twink made goofy
baby bird faces).

Mom and Dad
stay up late
into the night
whispering.

I tell Rose
I'm worried.
I'm worried my parents
are getting a divorce.

News

Mrs. Clifford claps
when I walk into
the classroom.
She calls out:
"Bravo, Diana!"
She hands me a letter.
The letter says
I have been invited
to join a poetry workshop
on the last week in July.
A famous city poet,
Mary Elmore DeMott,
will be teaching it.
It doesn't cost a penny.
Only ten students
were chosen
from the whole district.

I wish
I could feel happier.

Postcard

Dear Diana,

Congratulations on your poem.
I am proud of you.
I will write more
when my cold is better.

       Love,
          Grandpa Joe

GREETINGS FROM THE PLANETARIUM!

More Good News

My parents
are not
getting
a
divorce.

The Bad News

Dad announces: "I lost my job
last week."
Mom says, "We're short on
money now.
We'll have to cut back."
Cutting back means
no new bike
for my birthday.
I guess
I can live with that.

Twink to the Rescue

Twink brings her frog bank
to my room.
She empties it
on the rug.
"Help me count, Diana."
"Five dollars and
 sixty-three cents,"
I tell her.
She shouts: "I'm rich!"
She says: "I will
buy you a new bike
for your birthday!"

More Bad News

Grandpa Joe
fell off a ladder
and broke his arm.
He was trying to
clean the gutters
around his porch.
Mom will go visit.
She will stay
with Grandpa Joe
for a week
or two.

Ten Reasons Why Rose Is My Best Friend

1. When I told Rose I thought my parents
   might be getting a divorce, she didn't blab it
   all over the neighborhood.

2. When I told Rose that my dad lost his job
   and Grandpa Joe broke his arm, she hugged me.

3. Sometimes Rose lends me her purpy flopple.

4. Rose doesn't think I'm goofy because I love astronomy.
   (Boring maybe, but not goofy.)

5. Rose is nice to Twink. (Sometimes nicer than I am.)

6. Rose admits I'm better at Scrabble.

7. Rose listens to my poetry.

8. Rose lets me use her computer.

9. When I spilled a ten-pound bag of bird seed on the garage floor,
   Rose helped me clean it up.

10. Rose makes me laugh.

Care Package

We are fixing up
a care package
for Grandpa Joe.
Even Rose is helping.
Rose and I
make corn muffins.
Dad adds a bottle
of sparkling grape juice.
Twink puts in
three gum balls
and her stuffed rabbit,
George.
She asks me to help her
write a note
to go with George.
"Dear Grandpa Joe,
George is not to keep.
He is just to borrow
until your arm is better."

Music

Mom is the only one
in the house
who drinks tea.
I miss waking
to the old kettle
whistling
Mom's morning song.

Phone Call

Mom calls to say
that she and Grandpa Joe
are having a great time.
Grandpa is over
his cold.
He can still play chess—
with his right hand.
Mom says
Grandpa's porch
is screened in now.
No bugs.
You could even sleep there
in the summer
if you wanted to.
Mom says
there's a new playground
right down the road
from Grandpa's house.
And lots of kids my age.
I think to myself
it would be better
for Grandpa Joe
if there were
lots of people *his* age
in his neighborhood.
Twink whines.
She wants the phone.
She has to speak
to George.

Welcome Home, Mom

Finally
Mom is coming home.
It's been two weeks.
Twink and I hang
a WELCOME HOME banner.
(Can't disturb
the front-door Rice Krispies family.)
Rose made the banner
on her computer.

When we hear the car
we all run out.
Mom gives Twink
her George back.
Mom gives Dad a kiss.
She gives me a hug.

"I have some news,"
she says.

Uh-oh . . .
more news.

The Worst News of All

We are
going
to move.

Six Reasons Why We Have to Move

1. Because Dad lost his job.

2. Because we're short on money.

3. Because Grandpa Joe lives alone
   in a big, empty house.

4. Because Grandpa Joe wants to share
   his house with us.

5. Because I don't get a vote
   about moving.

6. Because even if I did, it would
   be three against one.

What About Snap, Crackle, and Pop?

Twink is happy.
She thinks moving
is a big adventure.
She twirls George around.
She sings: "We're moving! We're moving!"

"What about Snap, Crackle, and Pop?"
 I remind her.
"I'll tell Daddy to pack them up,"
 she says.
"You can't pack up birds."
"Mary Jo Dunbar packed up her bird
 when she moved."
"Mary Jo Dunbar's bird
 was a canary.
 Snap, Crackle, and Pop
 are wild birds.
 They'll have to stay here."

"Then I'll send them postcards."
 I roll my eyes at Twink.
"You know birds can't read."
"I know," she says.
"I'll ask the mailman
 to read to them."

Trying to Tell Rose

Today
I tried to tell Rose
that we are moving.
But before I could get
the words out,
my eyes filled up
with tears
and I ran home.

After School

Mrs. Clifford asks me
to stay after school.
She asks with a smile,
so I know I'm not in trouble.
When everyone is gone
Mrs. Clifford sits down with me.
"You seem sad, Diana.
Everything okay?"

I burst into tears.
Mrs. Clifford takes my hand.
We both just sit there
until I stop crying.
"We have to move," I tell her.
"And I don't want to."

"Tell me more," she says softly.

More

I tell Mrs. Clifford
about Dad's job
and no money
and going to live
at Grandpa Joe's.
She nods.
"It's okay
  to be sad, Diana."

"And I'm mad too,"
  I say.
"I'm mad at Dad's company
  for letting him go.
I'm mad at Twink
  because she's so happy
  and already packing.
I'm mad because I don't
  get a vote about moving."

"It's okay
  to be mad, Diana."

"And I'm mixed up too.
  I love my grandpa Joe.
  He's fun to spend time with.
  And I know he's lonely
  in his big house.
  And I think: Maybe it won't
  be so bad.
  And then I think: Oh yes it will."

Mrs. Clifford squeezes my hand.
"It's okay
    to be mixed up, Diana."

When I leave school,
I feel a little better.
I even whistle back at
the Rice Krispies family
in our front door wreath.
I guess Mrs. Clifford would say:
"It's okay
    to feel a little better, Diana."

The Bird Family

The bird family
moves
before we do.
When I wasn't looking
Snap,
Crackle,
and Pop
learned to fly
and away they went.
Twink says
they will fly across
the entire state
to visit us
at Grandpa Joe's.

May 31st

Today is my birthday.
Twink pops into my room.
"I wanted to buy you
 a bike."
"I know."
"It costed too much."
"I know."
"I got you
 a different present."
"Thank you, Twink."
"I wrapped it
 all by myself."
"I can see that."
"It's George!"
"You're giving me
 George?"
"No, I'm loanding
 you George."
"Wow! When do you
 want him back?"
"Tonight."
"I see."
"Happy birthday, big sister!"

More Birthday Gifts

From Mom—a batch of brownies
in a star-covered tin,
all mine.
I can keep them in my room.
Away from Twink.

From Dad—twenty dollars.
The start of my new-bike fund.

From Grandpa Joe—a poster of
the Horsehead Nebula.
And a moon-shaped bank.

From Rose—the purpy flopple.
So I will never forget her.
(As if I could.)

An Idea

Rose says
she is tired of crying.
Tired of thinking about
all the ways she is going to
miss me.
"I have an idea,"
I tell her.
"Make a list
of all the things
you won't miss about me."

Rose's List

1. I won't miss all your sky talk.
Nebula this. Sunspot that.

2. I won't miss your winning
every single Scrabble game.

3. I won't miss reading your diary.
Borrrr-ing.

4. I won't miss the way you
stuff your face with brownies.

5. I won't miss your booming burp
after you drink a can of soda.

6. I won't miss how you show my mom
your A's in science.

7. But I might miss . . . you

Wondering

Dad loves
the old shed
in the back garden.
He loves
puttering
among the flowerpots
and hand tools.
Sometimes
he brings his lunch
out there,
sits on the old
rickety stool.
Twink says
he's practicing
his jokes
on the spiders.
I say
he just likes
the quiet.
Twink says
that's dumb—
nobody likes quiet.
I say
I like quiet.
Sometimes.

I wonder—
will Dad miss
the quiet,
the shed,
the puttering?

The Last Night

This is my last night
in my room.
My bed frame
and mattress
lean against
the wall.
I'm lying
in Dad's old
sleeping bag
staring at
the blank spaces
where my astronomy charts
used to hang.
Tears spill
like crying stars
from my eyes.
I hear Twink
giggling at
one of Dad's
silly jokes.
Ha.
Ha. I'm
never
laughing
again.

Moving Day

I say my mad-sad good-byes.
Good-bye to my room
with the midnight blue walls
that look like night sky.
Good-bye to the yellow house
with the white shutters,
to the maple trees
and the daffodils
asleep in their beds.
Good-bye to Mrs. Clifford,
who stopped over
with a bag of
homemade cookies.

Good-bye to Rose,
who stands waving
as our car pulls off.

I watch her from the back window
until she is a tiny speck—
the hardest good-bye of all.

Grandpa Joe's House

Grandpa Joe's house
is white stucco
with a wide porch
and window boxes
overflowing with
geraniums.
There is the pine tree
I helped him plant
two years ago.
Grandpa points to a window.
"That's your room,"
he says.
"I had it painted
midnight blue.
Your astronomy posters
will look fine there."
This is Grandpa Joe's house.
This is where he lives.
Slowly
I carry my suitcase
up the front steps.

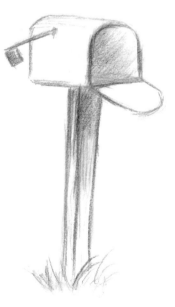

A Surprise

When I walk into
my new room
there is a balloon
tied to a chair.
It says WELCOME.
But that is not
the surprise
I'm talking about.
The surprise is
a brand-new
computer
sitting on the desk
that used to be
my mom's
when she was a girl.
Grandpa Joe stands
in the doorway
grinning.
"Now you can e-mail
your friend Rose
every day."

First Night

When you move
and go to sleep
for the first time
in a new room,
you feel strange.
Even if your new room
is midnight blue
like your old one.
Even if you are in
your own bed.
Even if your family
is in the same house.
Even if the same moon
that hung over
your old neighborhood
is hanging in
your new-neighborhood sky.
No matter what,
that first night
you feel strange,
spooky, and a little
lonely.

First Week

It's been a week
since we moved.
Today Dad told me a joke.
I faked a laugh.
Mom baked brownies—
my favorite.
I didn't eat a single one.
Grandpa Joe asked:
"Who wants to play chess?"
Twink, who doesn't know
a rook from a pawn,
piped: "Me!"

Everyone seems
to be trying to
make me feel better.
I don't *feel* like
feeling better.

Things I Miss About
Where I Used to Live

1. Playing Scrabble with Rose.

2. Reading diaries with Rose.

3. Reciting my poems to Rose.

4. Sleepovers at Rose's house.

5. Talking over my worries with Rose.

6. Trying to teach Rose about the sky.

7. Riding bikes with Rose.

8. Rose.

9. Rose.

10. Rose.

More Things I Miss

1. My old room.

2. Our maple tree.
(Grandpa's pine doesn't turn colors
in the fall and you can't climb it.)

3. Our kitchen.
(I knew where everything was.)

4. The Rice Krispies family.

5. Waking up happy.

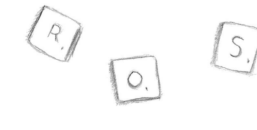

News Again

Dad got a job.
He's whooping.

Mom laughs.
Dances
around the kitchen
with Twink.

Grandpa Joe
opens a bottle
of sparkling grape juice
to celebrate.

I say:
"Does that mean
we can move back
home?"

The room goes silent.

Facing the Truth

Of course
we can't
move back.
I know that.
Our yellow house
has been sold.
To a family
with three kids
and two dogs.
This is my home now.
I sigh.
I pour myself
a glass of milk.
I ask Mom:
"Any of those
brownies left?"

Mail

Who could be sending me a letter?
Grandpa used to write to me,
but now that I live here
we just talk.
Rose and I e-mail each other,
so it can't be from her.
"Maybe it's from
  Mrs. Clifford," says Mom.
"Maybe it's from
  Snap, Crackle, and Pop!"
  says Twink.

The Letter

The letter is from
Mary Elmore DeMott,
the famous city poet.
It's about the poetry workshop.
She says I should bring
a thick notebook.
And pens.
And an idea
for a poetry project.
Grandpa Joe says:
"Maybe you can write
some poems
about moving."

July 27th

It's the morning
before the poetry workshop.
Mom is driving me
all the way there—
six hours from Pittsburgh.
I have my notebook
and pens.
I'm wearing
the purpy flopple.
I get itchy in the car.
Every mile I say:
"I'm nervous."
"I'm thirsty."
"I think I'm going to
  throw up."
"Are we there yet?"

It's like
I've turned into
Twink!

The Poetry Workshop

1.

Mary Elmore DeMott—
short blond hair,
green eyes,
swooshy red dress,
ballerina slippers—
begins.
She tells us:
be brave,
be messy,
write what we feel,
tell the truth,
love who we are,
share,
keep a notebook,
take it everywhere,
open our eyes
and our hearts.

2.

There are six of us
in the workshop.
Two boys.
Four girls.
Annie is the first
to share.
Her dad is
in the hospital.
Annie misses him
like crazy.
I know what it's like
to miss someone.
I read Annie my poem:
"Music,"
about Mom's teakettle.
I tell Annie about Rose.

3.

David tells the truth
to his friends.
He tells them:
"I write poems."
They tease him.
"But I love being
a poet,"
says David.
Mary Elmore DeMott smiles.
"You love who you are."

4.

Karen has a big family.
She says it's noisy
at her house.
Sometimes people argue,
play loud music.
Karen likes going
to the library,
writing her poems
in the quiet.
I think: We all need
quiet sometimes.
(Except for Twink.)

5.

Andy is the silly one.
He grabs the purpy flopple,
puts it on his head,
dances down the aisle.
He reads his
Pickle-Panda poem
aloud.
We all laugh so hard,
we are crying.
Even Mary Elmore DeMott.

6.

Joelle is very,
very
shy.
She doesn't talk much.
She doesn't read
her poems aloud.
Mary Elmore DeMott
reads Joelle's poems
to us.
They are beautiful.
Joelle apologizes
for not being brave.
Mary Elmore DeMott says:
"You're wrong, Joelle.
You were very brave
to come this week."

Another Good-bye

It's been a while since I've felt like I belong
somewhere.
The workshop is over.
We all say good-bye.
Mine is the hardest.
The others
live near one another,
but I'm six hours away.
They promise to keep in touch.
My heart feels like
an egg about to
crack.
I tell Mary Elmore DeMott.
She says: "Write that in
your notebook, Diana."

Homecoming

When Mom and I go
back "home"
Twink is waiting
at the door.
She runs out
waving a sheet of paper—
probably for Mom.
So I'm totally surprised
when Twink
jumps up and down
in front of me
screaming:
"Diana, I wroted you
a poem!"

Poem Composed by Twink
As Dictated to Grandpa Joe

You are my big sister.
I like you the bestest
of any big sister
in the whole world.
I missed you.
Love, Twink
PS: You said a poem doesn't have to rhyme.

Looking for Poems in
My New Neighborhood

I take my notebook outside
to the hot August day:
to Mr. Barr's dog, Tucker,
who likes to lick my knees . . .
to Mrs. Martin's gazebo,
painted pink as
strawberry ice cream . . .
to the tasseled weeds
in the lot near the old church . . .
to the donut shop with the blue door . . .
to the copper beech tree that's nearly
one hundred years old . . .
I take out my pencil.
I open my notebook
and my heart.

Perseids

I'm lying on my back
in the front yard
looking up at
the night sky,
looking for
shooting stars.

A voice—
a boy's voice—
says: "They're called
Perseids."

"Huh?" I say.

He repeats,
"Perseids.
The shooting stars
of August."

I sit bolt
upright,
my eyes wide
as moons—
"You know that?"

The Boy

His name is Sam Peter Ling.
He loves astronomy
as much as
I do.

His father has
a telescope.
They go to
star parties.

Sam says
I can come along
sometime.

I ask him:
"Do you like
to play Scrabble?"

He answers:
"Does Saturn
have rings?"

Five Reasons Why I Like Sam Peter Ling

1. He knows more about the night sky than anyone I've ever met.

2. He doesn't challenge me when I spell out the word *nebula* on the Scrabble board.

3. He listens to my poems.

4. He likes my poems.

5. He makes the best brownies.

Five Reasons Why Sam Peter Ling and I
Can't Really Be Best Friends

1. He's a boy.
2. He's a boy.
3. He's a boy.
4. He's a boy.
5. He's a boy.

Sam Replies to That List With a List of His Own

1. So what?
2. So what?
3. So what?
4. So what?
5. So what?

A Chat With Mom

Mom says:
"I like Sam."
I say:
"So do I."
Mom says:
"Sounds like there's
a problem."
I say:
"There is.
Sam's a boy."
Mom says:
"So what?"

A New Bike

Finally
I've got a new bike.
I forked over all
my savings, and Dad added the rest.
It's purple
to match
the purpy flopple.
Twink is monkey-faced.
"I was saving to buy you
a bike," she grumps.
"Now you went and got one!
And it's not even your birthday!
You cheated!"
Twink is crying.
I feel rotten.
I think. . . .
"Twink," I say.
"You can buy me something—
a basket for my bike.
So I can carry my Scrabble
game to Sam's
and my poetry notebook
everywhere!"
Twink cheers, "Yes!"
and runs to get
her frog bank.

This Is Where I Live

This is where I live.
In the white stucco house.
With the window boxes
and the red geraniums
and the fireflies blinking
against the darkening sky.
I look out my window.
I see my friend Sam
waving.
"Wanna go to a star party?"
he calls.
The moon is soft,
shimmery.
The sky so full of stars,
I could shower in them.
My heart is happy.
It's a good life when
the sky is twinkling
and the moon is pale
and Sam and I have plans.